# Yes, Dear

## A Comedy in One Acts

## by Warren Graves

A SAMUEL FRENCH ACTING EDITION

## STORY OF THE PLAY

Youthful parents suddenly feel old when they realise that their children are now adults. This is what happens to John and Marie Grant while they are preparing for the twenty-first birthday party of their daughter. In the privacy of their bedroom, John reverts to the clown he was as a young man and sweeps Marie along with him into the sheer zest of being alive. They realise that, for each other, they will always be the same. This is a charming and very funny family comedy.

# DESCRIPTION OF CHARACTERS

JOHN GRANT: (46) We meet John in his dress trousers and undervest giving full reign to his comic imagination. As the play progresses, and he dresses, we are able to realise that we have seen a very successful captain of industry letting his hair down to protect himself and his wife against the thought of advancing age. He is the father of a very happy family.

MARIE GRANT: (42) Marie is used to John's horse-play and much depends on her non-reaction at the outset. Having confessed what is bothering her, she relaxes and allows John to lead her wherever he feels they should go.

DEE GRANT: (21) Dee is just getting used to being an adult and reproves her parents at the adult level. Her "spanking" indicates that she can be an adult but she is also their daughter. She agrees, happily, and their new relationship is now established.

## CLOTHING

This plays an important part in this drama. Both John and Marie start in their underwear and subsequently, when they are dressed, polished and immaculate, we feel we know them a lot better than many of their friends. We have intruded into an area where only they know each other. Dee should work the other way. She should be stunning enough for her spanking to come as a slight shock. Her reaction and the exchange of abuse with her father reveal that she is only just out of daughter and into womanhood.

# CHARACTERS

John Grant

Marie Grant

Dee Grant


# SCENE

*The bedroom of John and Marie Grant.*

# Yes, Dear



Scene: *The action takes place in the bedroom of John and Marie Grant as they prepare for the twenty-first birthday party of their daughter Dee. Bedroom door D. L., bathroom door (open throughout) D. R. Marie is seated at dressing table, R. when the Curtain rises. She is dressed in a slip and is making up her eyes. Beside the bathroom door Upstage is a chest on which is a box of kleenex; beyond that is a double bed, bedside table and transistor radio. Center back, draped window, to the R. of which is a fitted wardrobe. The room is tastefully furnished, indicating the Grants are people of some substance. The only incongruous note in the room is a highways STOP sign beside the bed.*

John. (*Off, in bathroom.*) FEEgaro—figaro, figaro, figaro. Figaro here—figaro there—figaro here, figaro there, figaro here, figaro there— Here a figaro—there a figaro, everywhere a figaro E-I-E-I-O. (*Pause.*) Serheventy-six trombones led the big parade, seventy-six oh hell. (John, *in trousers and undershirt, swings the top half of his body into the room, one hand shielding his eyes. He scans the room.*) Kleenex!

Marie. On the chest.

(John *sees the box right next to him, flicks out a tissue, dabs his cheek, looks at it, re-acts and swings back into the bathroom. A pause.*)

John. Marie!

Marie. Yes, dear.

John. Did you know that some of the crowned heads of Europe were haemophilic?

MARIE. (*Mumbles.*) I didn't know that.

JOHN. What?

MARIE. I said I didn't know that.

JOHN. Well, we are. Just one little nick shaving and we bleed to death—nothing anybody can do about it.

MARIE. Is that right?

JOHN. (*Mutters inaudibly, then.*) I'm going, Marie.

MARIE. Goodbye, dear.

JOHN. The king is dead—long live the king. (*Pompomming the "Dead March," he enters wearing the bath towel as a train, collects his shirt and returns majestically to the bathroom.*)

MARIE. (*After a pause.*) John.

JOHN. Yes, dear.

MARIE. Are my ear-rings in there?

JOHN. Yes, dear.

MARIE. Bring them in, will you?

JOHN. Not now, dear—I'm dying. (MARIE *rises impatiently and enters the bathroom. There is a SLAP, a yelp from* JOHN, *and* MARIE *returns to the dressing table.* JOHN *appears in the doorway, towelling his face.*) You have hands like pineapples, madame.

MARIE. Hurry up and get ready.

JOHN. (*Looks at his* WIFE *for a few moments, then:*) You know something? You're not a bad-looking woman for an old bag. In fact I am this instant taken with your comeliness. What are you doing tonight?

MARIE. John, please! I promised Dee I would be down before her first guests arrived—you'd better be there too.

JOHN. Yes, dear.

MARIE. I'm late already . . . *you* are *very* late.

JOHN. Yes, dear.

MARIE. Now be a good boy and finish whatever it is you are doing in there because I want to come in.

JOHN. Yes, dear. (*He stands for a moment thoughtfully, beats silently on his chest, beats his towel over the head and drags it heavily back into the bathroom.*)

MARIE. What time is it?

JOHN. No idea.

MARIE. Well, my watch is in there.

JOHN. Where?

MARIE. On the thing.

JOHN. Oh . . . nearly twenty past seven. (JOHN *comes out of the bathroom doing up one cuff of an otherwise unbuttoned and flowing shirt. He moves to his* WIFE *and stands with his back to her. Coyly.*) Zip me up, will you?

(MARIE *ignores this, rises and moves to the bathroom.* JOHN *pursues her across the room, fencing furiously. She stops at the door and turns.* JOHN *is doing up his cuff.*)

MARIE. What is the matter with you this evening? Get ready. (*Exits into bathroom.*)

JOHN. Yes, dear. How about a little drink, would you like a little drink?

MARIE. (*Off.*) GET READY!

JOHN. I'd love a little drink. (*He goes to fitted cupboard and gets a bottle of sherry and one glass. He takes this to the dressing table and pours himself a drink. As he lifts it to his lips.*)

MARIE. (*Off.*) You've gone very quiet in there all of a sudden, what are you doing?

JOHN. You just told me to get ready.

MARIE. So?

JOHN. (*Sotto.*) That's just what I'm doing, lady—heh, heh.

MARIE. (*She enters, smoothing her dress.*) What's that?

JOHN. Sherry.

MARIE. Have you been downstairs like that?

JOHN. No. I had it hidden in the cupboard. This is a very good sherry . . . after I'd bought it, I couldn't stand the thought of all those gay young things mixing it with seven up—so I hid it in the cupboard.

MARIE. I'll have some when you've finished. Move off the table—I want to do my nails.

JOHN. No need to wait for me to finish my cabbage, I hid a glass for you too. (*Goes to get it.*) Romantic, isn't it—hiding a bottle and two glasses in your own bedroom?

MARIE. Were you going to lure one of Dee's friends up here during the party?

JOHN. (*Returning and pouring drink.*) What an excellent idea—I hadn't thought of that.

MARIE. Who do you fancy?

JOHN. Oh, I don't know—

MARIE. John! That's far too much. (*Takes it anyway.*)

JOHN. How about the go-go queen, what's her name— Ed and Amy's daughter?

MARIE. Barbara?

JOHN. Is it Barbara? The one with legs.

MARIE. My dear, they all have legs.

JOHN. I don't agree . . . they all have visible means of support but only a couple have what I would call actual legs.

MARIE. You seem quite the expert. Have you reached that awkward age when you stare at girls' legs?

JOHN. My dear woman, I have been staring at girls' legs ever since I could get one eye over the side of my buggy. I must say the swinging cat seems to have more leg than I recall seeing before . . . ho hum . . . nevertheless, as one gets older one appreciates the finer things in life . . . like the way game improves after it has been hung for a while.

MARIE. (*Shocked.*) John!

JOHN. Yes, dear.

MARIE. You're terrible.

JOHN. Yes, dear.

MARIE. It worries me sometimes. You still seem very young, active— (JOHN *beats silently on his chest as before.*) even immature in some ways. I don't know how you do it.

JOHN. It isn't easy. Everybody wants me to grow up . . . even me. Sometimes I think they are right . . . then again, as Tinkerbelle and I flit homeward over the rooftops I say to myself--what the hell? Huh. Matter of fact, I don't think I can hold out much longer. Number one child having her twenty-first birthday comes as a bit of a shock. (*Slight pause, into Cassius Clay.*) But I will fight any time, any place, because I am the greatest, the fastest—

MARIE. Hardly the fastest.

JOHN. I will take you in five, five—

MARIE. Get ready.

JOHN. (*Shaping up.*) I'm ready. Make your move.

MARIE. What's the time?

JOHN. No idea.

MARIE. I'm sure we're late.

JOHN. How can we be late? We live here.

MARIE. I know, but I wish you'd hurry.

JOHN. Me hurry? You're sitting there doing nothing.

MARIE. I am not doing nothing. I am waiting for my nails to dry.

JOHN. (*Shuffles off to continue dressing.*) Huh. Nail varnish . . . lipstick . . . . powder, foundation cream, hair spray, eye shadow. Miss Ukranian Easter Egg nineteen-o-five. (MARIE *sniffs.*) You're crying.

MARIE. I am *not* crying! (*She sniffs again.*)

JOHN. You are crying. I can tell. I'm sorry.

MARIE. Sorry I'm crying or sorry what you said?

JOHN. Both. This is supposed to be a joyful occasion. The beautiful Dee is a woman today and— (MARIE *sniffs very loudly.*) Whadisay! Whadisay!?

MARIE. Look.

JOHN. What?

MARIE. Look in the mirror.

JOHN. Where?

MARIE. In there. That's me.

JOHN. Are you being symbolic?

MARIE. Yes. That's me. That's what I see.

JOHN. So?

MARIE. Well, she could hardly compete with a go-go queen, could she?

JOHN. Compete with a go-go queen?! I should damn well hope not. (*Points into mirror.*) That lady happens to be the wife of a very respectable businessman in this community and she doesn't watusi, jerk, frug, and everybody is very happy about it—particularly her husband. Mind you, I have seen her practising the bump and grind when she thought nobody was looking, but she—

MARIE. You haven't.

JOHN. I have.

MARIE. When?

JOHN. You remember a couple of Thursdays back I was home early—I arrived bellowing "Hullo, Marie—I'm home—yoo hoo"?

MARIE. Yes?

JOHN. Well, I'd been in once already. I saw you cavorting about up here in your undergarments, so I went out and came in again. "Hullo, Marie—yoo hoo."

MARIE. Oh, John.

JOHN. Oh, Marie.

MARIE. What must you have thought?

JOHN. I thought you were very good.

MARIE. (*Pleased.*) Really?

JOHN. Very good indeed. That's what gave me the idea about the sherry. I thought if I could pour enough of that down you—

MARIE. (*Realization.*) How dare you go sneaking round the house when I think you are out!

JOHN. (*Sings.*) "You see a pair of laughing eyes—whizz boom, and suddenly you're sighing sighs, whizz boom."

MARIE. (*Laughs with embarrassment, covering her face. She recovers, smiling. Softly.*) John?

JOHN. Yes, dear.

MARIE. (*Holds out her hand.*) Come here.

(JOHN *takes her hand. She draws him down to sit on the floor beside the dressing table stool.*)

JOHN. What's up?

MARIE. Do you know I'm frightened?

JOHN. Frightened? Why?

MARIE. Silly. My little girl—my baby—twenty-one today. Twenty-one. It doesn't seem possible, surely it's not possible.

JOHN. I'm afraid it is.

MARIE. I know. Are you proud of her, John—are you pleased with her?

JOHN. She's very beautiful—just like her mother.

MARIE. Well, thank you, kind sir.

JOHN. I mean it, dammit. One of the most difficult things a husband can do in a marriage is to pay his wife a compliment. Every time I say—

MARIE. (*Puts her finger on his lips.*) Sssh!

JOHN. Sorry.

MARIE. You're right. She is lovely—and she is a woman—and I am her mother. Oh, John John John—how old does that make me? You have no idea what I feel when I realise that my own daughter is a woman. I look at Dee and think "she can't be like that. She's only a baby. I'm more like that than she is." Do you know something? Every now and then I have the extraordinary feeling that I can step back and look at all of us from the outside. Do you know what I mean? I'm like somebody else. I see you—and me—and Dee, and the boys and it's all so—*reliable*. Then I suddenly realise that the woman I am looking at is me—and I can't believe it. I don't know if this makes any sense at all, but—I *still* don't feel ready for the responsibilities of marriage and raising a family . . . I'm not clever enough . . . I'm not old enough. Can you understand that?

JOHN. Yes. I think I can.

MARIE. Honestly?

JOHN. Know something?

MARIE. What?
JOHN. It's just the same for me.

(*Pause.*)

MARIE. (*Some sadness.*) I think we ought to have another sherry.
JOHN. (*Brightens.*) Sound thinking, Mrs. Grant. (*Rises.*) I don't think we should worry about it. By the time we're both ready—it could be all over. (*Pouring drinks.*) I shall know exactly how the business should be run the day after I retire. How to raise children properly will occur to me when I see how badly my grandchildren are being brought up. Right now—I just wouldn't know. And I'm supposed to be at the helm. Take sex.
MARIE. Not now, dear, we really are very late.
JOHN. I take it you instructed your daughter correctly. (*Hands her drink.*)
MARIE. Thank you. Your health.
JOHN. Likewise.
MARIE. I think she was way ahead of me.
JOHN. Same with me and the boys—about the mechanics anyway. But what about the social side—the day-to-day battle of the sexes? What makes boys and girls interested in each other, anyway? I think they should ask some old man who has forgotten his own experiences and can talk straight from the head.
MARIE. Perhaps they think you are some old man who has forgotten.
JOHN. I drink to forget.
MARIE. Does it help?
JOHN. (*Leers.*) You're joking, of course.
MARIE. (*Laughing.*) So what do we do?
JOHN. Nothing. Absolutely nothing. Just carry on to the best of our ability, hope that we're right and that it will all work out in THE END.
MARIE. Perhaps you're right. What's the time?

JOHN. Oh, for God's sake, go and get your watch off the thing, will you?

MARIE. Oh, yes. (*She exits and returns immediately.*) It's quarter past eight, you know.

JOHN. No, I didn't know.

MARIE. We really ought to—

JOHN. We shall go downstairs when we are calm and composed as befits our advanced years. I don't feel ready to descend into the maelstrom of youth and act with proper dignity. If the balance of nature is to be preserved, Daddy has to behave like a— (*Draws square with index fingers.*) Unfortunately, Daddy isn't a square. In fact I'd say I was cooking. Let's have another drink.

MARIE. I don't think we should. (*He draws square again.*) Well, just one.

JOHN. Let's play a game.

MARIE. (*Weakly.*) A game?

JOHN. Yes. Let's play knock, knock. Do you know how to play knock, knock?

MARIE. I think so.

JOHN. Good. I'll start. Knock, knock.

MARIE. Come in.

JOHN. Omigod! No. I say "Knock, knock," and then you say "Who's there?" and then I say something like "Elvis" or "Fred," and you say "Elvis or Fred who?" and I say something very funny indeed and you laugh and then it's your turn, okay? Right. Knock, knock.

MARIE. Who's there?

JOHN. Jasper.

MARIE. Come in—no—Jasper who?

JOHN. Jasper song at twilight. Ho ho ho, deary me— you messed that up, didn't you? Never mind, try another one. Knock, knock.

MARIE. Who's there?

JOHN. Ferdinand.

MARIE. Ferdinand who?

JOHN. Ferdinand worth two in bush—what a riot the man is. Now you try one.

MARIE. I don't think I could.
JOHN. Sure you can. Shut your eyes and jump in.
MARIE. Oh, all right. Knock knock.
JOHN. Who's there?
MARIE. Marvin.
JOHN. Marvin? Are you sure?
MARIE. (*Indignant.*) That's not what you're supposed to say.
JOHN. Sorry, sorry. Marvin who?
MARIE. Marvindow von't open.
JOHN. (*Prof. Higgins.*) By George, she's got it. I do believe she's got it. Now we'll dance.
MARIE. (*Laughs.*) Dance?
JOHN. (*Skips to the bedside table and produces a transistor RADIO, switches it on and it is playing Frank Sinatra singing "The Tender Trap." JOHN yells.*) They're playing our tune!

(*He moves in front of the bed and starts the disinterested gum-chewing two step of a Fairground chorine. MARIE joins him, slowly, with the bump and grind. There is a KNOCK at the door.*)

MARIE. (*Gaily.*) Knock, knock.
JOHN. (*Gaily.*) Who's there? (*They stop dead. Who is there? JOHN leaps to the RADIO and switches it off. MARIE nervously touches her hair and smooths her dress. JOHN returns to the front of the bed. When they are composed:*) Come in.

(DEE *enters* R.)

DEE. Mummy, Daddy—what on earth are you doing?
JOHN. Er—dancing?
DEE. *Dancing!*
JOHN. Yes. A little thing called the creaking back. I don't think your group has got round to it yet.
DEE. Daddy! You've been drinking.
JOHN. This is true. You see my daughter is twenty-one

today and, although I would like to celebrate her independence, I'm just a little shattered by the whole thing. Her mother is also shattered.

DEE. All the same, I think it's unfair of you to hide away up here enjoying yourselves when I'm downstairs going frantic.

JOHN. Enjoying ourselves? Enjoying ourselves! My dear girl, you suddenly confront us wth the breaking up of a perfectly good family and then you accuse us of enjoying ourselves. Don't you know what day this is?

DEE. It's my twenty-first birthday.

JOHN. It is like hell your birthday. Today is the beginning of the end. We've been luckier longer than most maybe, but any day now you are going to take off from this little nest and go into the big bad world. I've been expecting it since you were eighteen, but this is it. My sons will be next. You're all going to run out before the mortgage. Three empty bedrooms at a hundred and ten a month staring me in the face. Your mother and I moving silently among the furniture touching things—trying to remember what it was we used to talk about before we had any children.

DEE. Oh, Daddy, don't be so dramatic.

JOHN. You can call me John.

DEE. I don't want to call you John.

JOHN. Aha. Want to play both ends against the middle, eh? One foot in the world and one in the womb? Well that can be pretty dangerous. The sooner you learn the difference between a Daddy and a John— (*He breaks off; that didn't come out right.*)

MARIE. (*Picks up cue very quickly.*) I don't think you're being very fair about this. She can't help being twenty-one.

JOHN. What time did it happen?

MARIE. What?

JOHN. At what precise moment did you introduce this creature into what had been, up until then, a very well-ordered life?

MARIE. Do you mean when was she born?

JOHN. I do. What time.

MARIE. Ten o'clock—at night.

JOHN. Aha. (*Swings out dressing table stool into* c. *and sits on it. To* DEE.) Come and sit on Daddy's knee.

DEE. (*Apprehensive.*) What for?

JOHN. Something special . . . your old daddy just wants a word with you. Come along.

(DEE *approaches. When she is within grasp,* JOHN *grabs her and swings her over his knee.*)

DEE. (*Shrieks.*) Daddy!

JOHN. (*Digs his fingers into her back and she squeals with laughter.*) Be quiet. Marie, pass me the hair brush.

MARIE. Surely you're not going to—?

JOHN. Pass me the hair brush, woman, or you're next. (MARIE *does so.*) Now then, milady, I am still monarch of all I survey until ten o'clock. I've never done this before— (*Whack with the brush.*) did that hurt?

DEE. No.

JOHN. Well fake it.

DEE. (*Bellows.*) W-a-a-a!

JOHN. Beautiful. Now we have some scores to settle. This first one is for spoiling a beautiful evening when your mother and I were at a concert. You decided to arrive.

MARIE. We were at a movie.

JOHN. A concert sounds better and she gets it anyway. (*Whack.*)

DEE. W-a-a-a!

JOHN. This one is for having the measles the first time I had saved enough money for a proper holiday at a hotel. (*Whack.*)

DEE. (*Says.*) Groan, groan.

JOHN. The next request I have here tonight comes from a Mr. and Mrs. Grant. You subjected two perfectly happy people to the boring game of mothers and fathers and stretched it out for over twenty years. (*Whack.*)

DEE. The pain—the pain.

JOHN. Now sit up properly. (DEE *does so.*) Wild horses wouldn't drag it out of me, of course, but your mother and I are just the kind of people who enjoy this sort of boredom. We're masochists. We wouldn't have missed one measle spot, one pop record or one late night wondering where the hell you were. We love you—happy birthday—I now pronounce you well and truly launched and God help those you sail into.

DEE. I ought to say something.

JOHN. How about saying to your mother that you don't need her downstairs? Tell her one of her old boy friends wants to take her to a party.

DEE. (*Thinks, then kisses him swiftly.*) Okay.

(*She goes to her* MOTHER *and they embrace.*)

JOHN. (*Fondly.*) Well look at that now—makes you sick, doesn't it? Go on, get off downstairs with you.

DEE. (*Moving to door.*) Don't you be long now.

MARIE. We'll be right down.

DEE. (*At door.*) I hope I don't get a husband as crazy as you. (*And out.*)

JOHN. (*Calling.*) Who wants a girl with freckles!

(MARIE *sits at the bed, watching* JOHN *pick up his jacket, brush the sleeves and slowly puts it on. She is smiling. He is frowning.*)

MARIE. (*Eventually.*) You look handsome. (JOHN *bows.*) Are you ready?

JOHN. I think so.

MARIE. "Calm and composed as befits our advanced years"?

JOHN. (*Smiles.*) Enough to fool some of the people most of the time. Maybe it's enough. (JOHN *moves to his*

Wife *and offers her his arm. She rises, takes it and they move slowly to the door.*) Downstairs we shall be confronted with a heaving mass of young energy quite terrifying to behold. Don't be alarmed by its intensity, and don't be afraid. Remember, you are with me.

Marie. Yes, dear.

(John *opens the door, and* Marie *exits. He watches her pass. The noise of the PARTY can be heard: "Tender Trap" almost inaudible. He looks back into the room.*)

John. (*Whispers, with actions.*) Whizz boom.

(*He flicks off LIGHT. Fade up PARTY, fade up "Tender Trap" and:*)

### THE CURTAIN FALLS

# PROPERTY PLOT

*Bathroom (Off):*
  Ear-rings
  Bath towel
  Face towel
  Wristwatch (Marie)

*Chest:*
  Kleenex

*Easy Chair:*
  Shirt (John)

*Cupboard:*
  Jacket of dress suit
  Bow tie
  Sherry
  Two glasses

*Bedside Table:*
  Transistor radio

*Dressing Table:*
  Assorted cosmetics
  Mascara
  Eye-liner
  Nail polish
  Nail varnish
  Lipstick
  Tissues
  Brushes
  John's studs

# ELECTRICS

The scene is inside at night and it is essential that soft lighting instil an intimate atmosphere. One harsh light comes from the bathroom. Other light sources are from the dressing table, tri-lite and occasional lamp (on chest). Dark shadow at the back of the stage would enhance the effect.

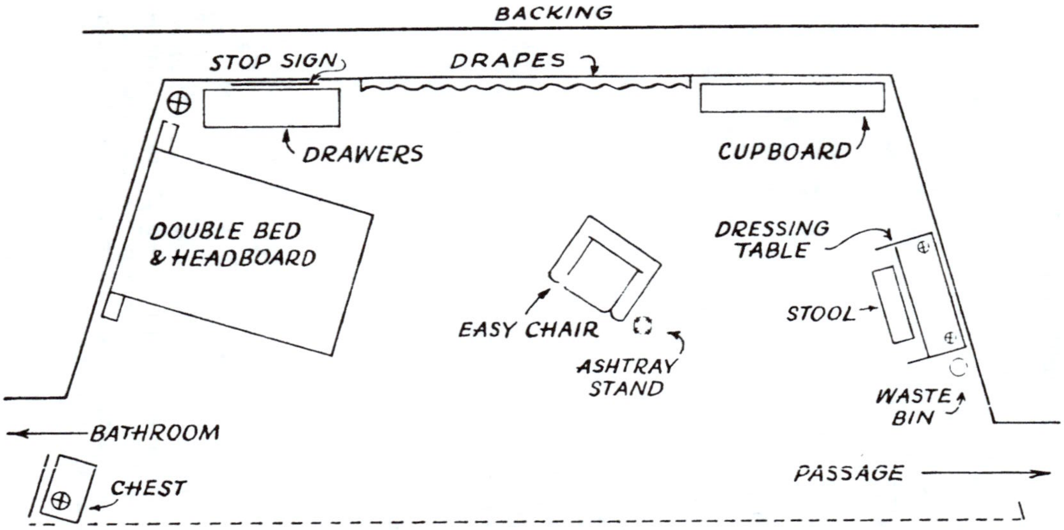

SCENE DESIGN
"YES, DEAR"

## SKIN DEEP
### Jon Lonoff

*Comedy / 2m, 2f / Interior Unit Set*

In *Skin Deep*, a large, lovable, lonely-heart, named Maureen Mulligan, gives romance one last shot on a blind-date with sweet awkward Joseph Spinelli; she's learned to pepper her speech with jokes to hide insecurities about her weight and appearance, while he's almost dangerously forthright, saying everything that comes to his mind. They both know they're perfect for each other, and in time they come to admit it.

They were set up on the date by Maureen's sister Sheila and her husband Squire, who are having problems of their own: Sheila undergoes a non-stop series of cosmetic surgeries to hang onto the attractive and much-desired Squire, who may or may not have long ago held designs on Maureen, who introduced him to Sheila. With Maureen particularly vulnerable to both hurting and being hurt, the time is ripe for all these unspoken issues to bubble to the surface.

"Warm-hearted comedy … the laughter was literally show-stopping. A winning play, with enough good-humored laughs and sentiment to keep you smiling from beginning to end."
- TalkinBroadway.com

"It's a little Paddy Chayefsky, a lot Neil Simon and a quick-witted, intelligent voyage into the not-so-tranquil seas of middle-aged love and dating. The dialogue is crackling and hilarious; the plot simple but well-turned; the characters endearing and quirky; and lurking beneath the merriment is so much heartache that you'll stand up and cheer when the unlikely couple makes it to the inevitable final clinch."
- NYTheatreWorld.Com

## TREASURE ISLAND
Ken Ludwig

*All Groups / Adventure / 10m, 1f (doubling) / Areas*
Based on the masterful adventure novel by Robert Louis Stevenson, *Treasure Island* is a stunning yarn of piracy on the tropical seas. It begins at an inn on the Devon coast of England in 1775 and quickly becomes an unforgettable tale of treachery and mayhem featuring a host of legendary swashbucklers including the dangerous Billy Bones (played unforgettably in the movies by Lionel Barrymore), the sinister two-timing Israel Hands, the brassy woman pirate Anne Bonney, and the hideous form of evil incarnate, Blind Pew. At the center of it all are Jim Hawkins, a 14-year-old boy who longs for adventure, and the infamous Long John Silver, who is a complex study of good and evil, perhaps the most famous hero-villain of all time. Silver is an unscrupulous buccaneer-rogue whose greedy quest for gold, coupled with his affection for Jim, cannot help but win the heart of every soul who has ever longed for romance, treasure and adventure.

**THE OFFICE PLAYS**
Two full length plays by Adam Bock

**THE RECEPTIONIST**
*Comedy / 2m, 2f / Interior*

At the start of a typical day in the Northeast Office, Beverly deals effortlessly with ringing phones and her colleague's romantic troubles. But the appearance of a charming rep from the Central Office disrupts the friendly routine. And as the true nature of the company's business becomes apparent, The Receptionist raises disquieting, provocative questions about the consequences of complicity with evil.

"...Mr. Bock's poisoned Post-it note of a play."
*- New York Times*

"Bock's intense initial focus on the routine goes to the heart of
*The Receptionist's* pointed, painfully timely allegory... elliptical,
provocative play..."
*- Time Out New York*

**THE THUGS**
*Comedy / 2m, 6f / Interior*

The Obie Award winning dark comedy about work, thunder and the mysterious things that are happening on the 9th floor of a big law firm. When a group of temps try to discover the secrets that lurk in the hidden crevices of their workplace, they realize they would rather believe in gossip and rumors than face dangerous realities.

"Bock starts you off giggling, but leaves you with a chill."
*- Time Out New York*

"... a delightfully paranoid little nightmare that is both more
chillingly realistic and pointedly absurd than anything
John Grisham ever dreamed up."
*- New York Times*

SAMUELFRENCH.COM

## NO SEX PLEASE, WE'RE BRITISH
Anthony Marriott and Alistair Foot

*Farce / 7 m, 3 f / Interior*

A young bride who lives above a bank with her husband who is the assistant manager, innocently sends a mail order off for some Scandinavian glassware. What comes is Scandinavian pornography. The plot revolves around what is to be done with the veritable floods of pornography, photographs, books, films and eventually girls that threaten to engulf this happy couple. The matter is considerably complicated by the man's mother, his boss, a visiting bank inspector, a police superintendent and a muddled friend who does everything wrong in his reluctant efforts to set everything right, all of which works up to a hilarious ending of closed or slamming doors. This farce ran in London over eight years and also delighted Broadway audiences.

"Titillating and topical."
- "NBC TV"

"A really funny Broadway show."
- "ABC TV"

**ANON**
Kate Robin

*Drama / 2m, 12f / Area*

Anon. follows two couples as they cope with sexual addiction. Trip and Allison are young and healthy, but he's more interested in his abnormally large porn collection than in her. While they begin to work through both of their own sexual and relationship hang-ups, Trip's parents are stuck in the roles they've been carving out for years in their dysfunctional marriage. In between scenes with these four characters, 10 different women, members of a support group for those involved with individuals with sex addiction issues, tell their stories in monologues that are alternately funny and harrowing..

In addition to Anon., Robin's play What They Have was also commissioned by South Coast Repertory. Her plays have also been developed at Manhattan Theater Club, Playwrights Horizons, New York Theatre Workshop, The Eugene O'Neill Theater Center's National Playwrights Conference, JAW/West at Portland Center Stage and Ensemble Studio Theatre. Television and film credits include "Six Feet Under" (writer/supervising producer) and "Coming Soon." Robin received the 2003 Princess Grace Statuette for playwriting and is an alumna of New Dramatists.

## **WHITE BUFFALO**
Don Zolidis

*Drama / 3m, 2f (plus chorus)/ Unit Set*
Based on actual events, WHITE BUFFALO tells the story of the
miracle birth of a white buffalo calf on a small farm in southern
Wisconsin. When Carol Gelling discovers that one of the buffalo
on her farm is born white in color, she thinks nothing more of
it than a curiosity. Soon, however, she learns that this is the ful-
fillment of an ancient prophecy believed by the Sioux to bring
peace on earth and unity to all mankind. Her little farm is quickly
overwhelmed with religious pilgrims, bringing her into contact
with a culture and faith that is wholly unfamiliar to her. When a
mysterious businessman offers to buy the calf for two million dol-
lars, Carol is thrown into doubt about whether to profit from the
religious beliefs of others or to keep true to a spirituality she knows
nothing about.

# BLUE YONDER
## Kate Aspengren

*Dramatic Comedy / Monolgues and scenes*
*12f (can be performed with as few as 4 with doubling) / Unit Set*

A familiar adage states, "Men may work from sun to sun, but women's work is never done." In Blue Yonder, the audience meets twelve mesmerizing and eccentric women including a flight instructor, a firefighter, a stuntwoman, a woman who donates body parts, an employment counselor, a professional softball player, a surgical nurse professional baseball player, and a daredevil who plays with dynamite among others. Through the monologues, each woman examines her life's work and explores the career that she has found. Or that has found her.

www.ingramcontent.com/pod-product-compliance
Lightning Source LLC
Chambersburg PA
CBHW070423120726
47909CB00005B/1776